Herb Fairies

A Magical Tale of Plants & Their Remedies

When four young friends discover an herb fairy at the park, they are drawn into an adventure beyond their wildest dreams. The Old Man of the Forest has cast a terrible spell, locking up much of the plant magic in the world. The Herb Fairies turn to the children for help, and everyone discovers that the only way to restore the magic is by working together. By the end of this thirteen book series, readers become keepers of plant medicine magic.

Join the Herb Fairies Book Club!

Herb Fairies is a complete herbal learning system for kids.
For each of the thirteen books in the Herb Fairies series...

Draw and write about what you learned in your very own Magic Keeper's Journal.	Make the herbal remedies and recipes the kids make in the books with Recipe Cards!	Learn with puzzles, stories, songs, recipes, poems and games in Herbal Roots zine.	Color your favorite fairies or print out posters to hang on your bedroom wall.

Book club membership gives you access to the complete learning system on our mobile optimized site. Also includes audio books read by Kimberly, printable books and eBook versions for Kindle, iPad and other devices.

Visit **HerbFairies.com**

LearningHerbs

Herb Fairies
Book Thirteen:
Healing the Heart of the Forest

Written by Kimberly Gallagher
Illustrated by Swapan Debnath
Produced by John M. Gallagher

If you are not sure what a word means or how it is pronounced, check the glossary in the back of the book.

Special Thanks to my mom, Cheryl Delmonte, a fellow writer, who has always encouraged my love for the craft of weaving stories for others to enjoy.

Special Thanks to Maryann Gallagher Agostin, Hailey Gallagher, Rowan Gallagher, Rosalee de la Forêt, and the LearningHerbs community.

The herbal and plant information in Herb Fairies is for educational purposes only. The information within the Herb Fairies books and activities are not intended as a substitute for the advice provided by your physician or other medical professional. Always consult with a health care practitioner before using any herbal remedy or food, especially if pregnant, nursing, or have a medical condition.

ISBN: 978-1-938419-39-3

Published by LearningHerbs.com, LLC, Shelton, WA.
LearningHerbs and Herb Fairies logos are registered trademarks of LearningHerbs.com, LLC.
Herb Fairies is a registered trademark of LearningHerbs.com, LLC.
First print edition, January 2017. Published and printed in the U.S.A. on FSC® certified paper.

The Herb Fairies series is dedicated to the memory of
James Joseph Gallagher, Sr.

For Rowan and Hailey...

CHAPTER 1
A Surprise Visit

"Here, look. You can just see the marshmallow shoots barely poking through the soil." Hailey was showing her friend Sarah all the new baby plants returning to her family's medicinal herb garden.

"Oh, I remember Althea, the marshmallow fairy!" said Sarah.

These two girls had been on many adventures to the Fairy Herb Garden together, and Althea was one of the fairies they'd made special friends with. The healing magic of the marshmallow plant had helped them to heal a dwarf magic keeper.

"It's so great that all the magic keepers are healed now, isn't it?" Hailey said.

"It sure is! Now the plants' healing powers are stronger than ever," Sarah agreed. "To me it seems really magical that these plants come back like this. I'd never guess there was a live plant below the soil."

"I know. In just a few months the marshmallow flowers will be above my head. All that plant energy has been stored in the roots all winter. Look over here," said Hailey. "The violets are blooming."

Sarah bent down to touch the pretty purple violet flower that Hailey was pointing out. "Remember the candied violet flowers that Viola made for us?" she asked.

"Oh, those were so good! Want to try making some? I think we have everything we need."

"That would be fun! Let's finish looking at the rest of the babies first though."

The two girls found some baby lady's mantle plants growing near the bigger plant, and there was new growth on the wormwood and sage.

"Hey, look. The lemon balm is already pretty tall," said Sarah. "Remember Melissa, the lemon balm fairy?"

"I loved her harp music," said Hailey. "It made me imagine such beautiful things. "This whole part of the garden will be full of lemon balm soon. Remember how Melissa had such a big, sprawling house?"

"Yep, and remember how small Tago and Dandy's houses were?" The adventurous plantain and dandelion fairies were hardly ever at home.

"Here's a dandelion flower!" said Sarah, noticing it growing among the lemon balm leaves.

"One of the first of the season!" said Hailey. She reached down to touch it and suddenly, there was Dandy himself. The dandelion fairy made his way out from among the dandelion and lemon balm leaves. "Dandy!" Hailey squealed with delight.

"Hello, Hailey," said Dandy, smiling his charming, dimpled smile. "Oh, and Sarah too," he said, noticing the older girl behind Hailey.

"It's great to see you," said Sarah. "Have you come for a visit?"

"Well, yes and no," said Dandy. "Of course, I'm happy to visit with you children, but I'm afraid I've come on a rather important mission, actually. We need your help again."

"Really?" said Hailey. "I thought all the magic keepers were healed."

"Oh, they are," said Dandy. "It's not them. It's...well, it's the Old Man of the Forest. He's not doing well at all. He's got a fever, and he's been having these nasty headaches. He says all his joints hurt and he limps around, when he moves at all. He says he feels really tired and weak. Even though we try to keep him well fed he's still losing weight. We're afraid we're going to lose him."

"Oh dear," said Hailey. "We've got to get to the Fairy Herb Garden right away. I'm sure we can help to heal him."

"You get Rowan," said Sarah. "I'll run and find Camie."

"We'll be right back, okay, Dandy?"

"I'll be here," he said. "Thank you!"

Hailey went inside to find her brother, and Sarah took off running down the street to Camie's house. The four friends always went on fairy adventures together, and Hailey and Sarah knew they would need all of them if they were going to heal the Old Man.

Rowan and Hailey found a backpack and packed up Rowan's invisibility cloak from the elves, Hailey's flower crown from the trolls, and some herb books, since they figured Sarah wouldn't have time to run home and get hers. "Let's take this one about dandelion," Hailey suggested. "Since Dandy found us, I bet we'll need dandelion medicine to heal the Old Man."

"Good idea," said Rowan, stowing the book in the pack with the others.

The two returned to the garden, and it wasn't long before Sarah and Camie came bursting through the back gate. The four friends smiled at each other. They were excited to be going to the Fairy Herb Garden again. They quickly made their way behind the apple tree, where Dandy was waiting next to the single  blooming dandelion flower within the lemon balm patch. When he saw they had all arrived, Dandy flew over them and sprinkled them with fairy dust from his dandelion seed wand.

The children felt the familiar tingling sensation as the fairy dust landed on their skin, and then the swirling wind began to shrink and transport them at the same time. When the wind settled, they found themselves standing in Dandy's simple dandelion plant home. Sunny yellow flowers peeked down at them from above and the smooth, toothed leaves of the dandelion plants surrounded them.

CHAPTER 2
Dandelion Medicine?

Dandy brought out some dandelion flower cookies and a plate of dandelion flower fritters with honey to dip them in. "The Old Man of the Forest is in his cabin deep in the Enchanted Forest. We've got a long walk ahead of us, so please eat some food before we go."

Camie took a cookie from the tray. She'd had dandelion cookies before at Hailey's house, but she was excited to try these that Dandy himself had made. "Can't we just travel there using fairy dust?" she asked.

"Unfortunately, no," said Dandy. "That kind of travel doesn't work in the Enchanted Forest. We'll have to go on foot. Or on wing, in my case." He smiled and fluttered his dandelion leaf wings, making them ripple from his spine to their tips.

The children sat on the simple reed mats around Dandy's low table and enjoyed the cookies and fritters. They were glad for the snack before setting out. It hadn't been quite lunch time at home when Dandy found them.

"Wow! These are delicious," said Sarah, tasting one of the honey-dipped fritters. "I never knew you could eat dandelion flowers."

"Oh my gosh," said Hailey. "We love dandelion fritters and dandelion cookies. My mom makes soda from the flowers too! We look forward to dandelion season all winter."

Everyone ate quietly for a moment, enjoying the wonderful treats.

"I should tell you," said Dandy, "the Old Man of the Forest doesn't want help."

"What? Why not?" asked Sarah. "From your description, it seems like he's in really bad shape."

"He just keeps saying he deserves it, that he should have to suffer for what he did. No one's been able to talk any sense into him."

"It makes sense that he would have a hard time forgiving himself," said Rowan. "I know I do things I regret when I get angry, and that spell he cast sure did make a mess of things."

"I bet that's part of why he's sick," said Hailey. "Remember how Dad says emotions are often underneath our physical illnesses?"

"Yeah," said Rowan, "you're right. I bet Dad's acupuncture needles would help the Old Man."

"The herbs will help too," said Hailey.

"And maybe we can do something to help him forgive himself," said Camie.

"Yes," said Sarah. "I always feel better once other people forgive me." She'd stood up and was examining the dandelion leaf walls of Dandy's house. She found that she could always draw the plants better later if she examined them when she was fairy sized. She'd never thought of drawing a dandelion before, but now that she'd tasted the flowers, she thought they should go in her herb journal.

Hailey saw what she was doing and came over to her side. "Notice how the leaves are smooth all over?" she said.

"Yes," said Sarah.

"Well, there is a dandelion lookalike called cat's ear, but it has fuzzy leaves. That's one way you can tell them apart."

"See how dandelion leaves are toothed?" said Rowan. He pointed to the edges of the leaves. "That's how the plant got its name. *Dent de lion* is French for 'tooth of the lion.'"

"Wow! Really?" said Camie. "I didn't know that."

"What family do you think dandelion is in?" Hailey asked, pulling one of the flowers down so Sarah could look at it closely.

"Well, it's got lots of petals, like calendula, and the center looks like it could be made up of disc flowers. Is it an aster?"

"Yes!" Hailey smiled at her friend. Sarah had learned so much over their last year of Fairy Herb Garden adventures. "Since each petal is an individual flower, there are lots of dandelion seeds on this one flower head and they each have their own little parachute so they spread far and wide."

"My mom is always trying to get rid of the dandelions in our yard," said Sarah. "When we were little she used to pay us a quarter for every one we pulled up by the roots." She glanced sheepishly at Dandy as she said this, and was surprised to see a tear actually running down his cheek.

"Yeah," said Hailey, "but no matter how hard people try to get rid of them, dandelions just keep popping up. They bring so much good medicine to the people and they seem to know people need them. They don't stop offering their gifts."

"I bet now that the plant magic has been restored you'll see more and more lawns like ours," said Rowan. "Dandelion was the first plant my dad learned about as an herbalist. We have books and books about just that one plant and its healing qualities. Our parents even put up a sign in our yard that says *Dandelion Sanctuary*. That's started some interesting conversations with the neighbors."

"I had no idea dandelions had any healing qualities," said Sarah.

"Oh my gosh!" said Hailey. "Dandelions are just full of healing magic." She fished around in the backpack they'd brought until she found the dandelion book she and Rowan had packed. She handed it to Sarah, who sat down at the table with it.

After reading a few pages, Sarah looked up at Dandy. "I'm so sorry for all those plants I pulled," she said. "I didn't know..." Her voice trailed off and she dropped her eyes.

Dandy came over and gave Sarah a hug. "I know you didn't," he said. "But now the magic is all restored thanks to your efforts. Like Hailey said, more and more people will remember now." He gave her one of his most charismatic smiles.

"My mom told me they are even testing dandelion roots as an effective treatment for some kinds of cancer!" Hailey said.

"No way," said Camie. "Its medicine is that strong?"

"Uh-huh," said Hailey. "I'm sure it can help the Old Man of the Forest. We better do some gathering before we head to his cabin. I'd like to take some dried root with us, and do you have any flower-infused oil?" Hailey asked Dandy. "I think that will be good for his sore joints."

Dandy nodded and went to his kitchen to gather what Hailey asked for.

"Sarah, does it say anything in that book about how to use dandelion for a fever?" she asked. "I've never used it that way before."

Sarah began leafing through the book.

"I think we should gather lots of fresh dandelions too. The whole plants, roots and all. It sounds like the Old Man could use some powerful nourishment!"

"There's a place we can gather along the way," said Dandy.

"This book says the leaves can be used to reduce fever," said Sarah, "but it doesn't say how to prepare them."

"Hmmmm," said Hailey. She fished her flower crown out

of the backpack, and once it was settled on her head she felt confident suggesting they try a dandelion leaf tea for the fever. She asked Dandy for some dried dandelion leaves for making the tea.

Once they'd nestled all their supplies into the backpack, the little party set off to gather dandelions and journey into the Enchanted Forest.

CHAPTER 3
Harvesting Sunshine

Dandy took the children down a little hill to a nearby field, and as they approached it they gasped in wonder. Yellow flowers stretched out endlessly before them. Of course, they were still fairy sized, so when they reached the bottom of the hill they could only see the plants right around them, and the dandelion flowers were just above their heads. The children were glad when Dandy suggested he use his fairy magic to gather some whole plants. They knew it would take some time to dig dandelion roots even if they were human size. At fairy size it seemed like a very daunting task.

Dandy sprinkled fairy dust around the base of the plants and they simply emerged from the earth and lay waiting to be picked up. He did this four times with plants spaced some distance from each other so as not to leave a bare patch in the field. As he was doing this, the children gathered dandelion flowers and leaves, filling up a fairy basket with each one.

Hailey looked at the baskets of plant material and said, "Dandy, I think you better return us to our human size now. We're not going to be able to gather and carry enough plant material to heal the Old Man when we're fairy size."

So Dandy sprinkled them with fairy dust and they tingled a bit as they grew back to their human size. The fairy baskets they were holding grew with them and they were able to fill them with flowers, leaves, and the whole plants Dandy was gathering for them. They picked as they walked and found themselves talking and laughing happily  as they gathered. It was impossible not to feel joyful in that field of sunny yellow flowers. When they reached the other side of the field they looked back and were happy to see that despite their gathering, the field was still packed with healthy, flowering dandelion plants. They took a minute to give thanks for the plants they had gathered and the healing they knew they would bring, and then Dandy led them on into the Enchanted Forest.

As they walked along the forest trail, Rowan kept glancing from side to side and shaking his head. Hailey noticed and asked, "What is it, Rowan? What's wrong?"

"It's the forest," he said. "I thought it would feel healthy and vibrant now that the magic has been restored, but it feels dry and sad."

The other children stopped and looked around. They could see he was right. The forest felt even worse than it had on their previous walks through it.

"We think it's because the Old Man is so sick," said Dandy. "He's the heart of the forest, you know. So he's very important to its well-being."

"Are the elves still around, then, or have they moved to healthier areas?" Rowan asked.

"Oh, they're still here," said Dandy. "Even those that have left haven't found any healthier areas. The forest is in trouble and the elves are not in great shape either. Many of them are falling ill."

The children thought of their elf friends, Play, Knowledge, and Beauty, and moved forward with even more determination. They just had to heal the Old Man. They couldn't let the elves and forest die.

"Does he know?" Rowan asked.

"Does who know what?" asked Dandy.

"Does the Old Man know what his sickness is doing to the forest and the elves?"

"We haven't wanted to burden him with more guilt," said Dandy.

Rowan nodded and the little party walked solemnly on through the sick forest. It was a long way to the cabin, and their happy laughter in the sunny field of dandelion flowers seemed far behind them when they arrived at the Old Man's door.

They knocked and the May Queen opened the door for them. She looked tired and sad as she motioned them into the Old Man's room. He lay curled up on the bed with his face to the wall.

Sarah approached first, touching the Old Man gently on his shoulder. "We've come to help," she said, the soothing qualities of her voice even stronger since she was wearing the magical necklace the brownies had given her.

The Old Man rolled toward her, but he couldn't look into her eyes. "I don't want your help," he said. "I don't deserve it."

"I know you feel bad," said Sarah calmly. "We've all done things we wish we hadn't, and it's hard to forgive ourselves."

"But your sickness is affecting the whole forest!" said Rowan, unable to keep the anger and fear out of his voice.

"The elves are even starting to get sick. You have to let us help you."

At Rowan's words, the Old Man's eyes got big. He put his hand up to his forehead. "Ahhhhh. It's pounding!" he said. "I know. I know. I'm a terrible person. I can't do anything right." He sounded so defeated that Rowan's mood softened.

"It's going to be okay," said Sarah, quietly. "It's going to take courage to heal, to really face all that's happened. But you can do it. I know you can. You're strong, and you're important to the world. You can do this."

The Old Man reached for Sarah's hand and looked up into her eyes. He saw compassion there. Compassion and love and faith—these things became a lifeline for him. He looked over at Rowan and thought of all the children had done to help bring the magic back to the world. He realized he had a responsibility, a responsibility to the forest and the elves and to everyone. He couldn't allow himself to drown in his shame and grief. He looked back into Sarah's eyes. "Okay," he said. "Okay. I'll try."

CHAPTER 4
Healing

"That's the spirit!" said Dandy, grinning broadly.

Hailey came forward with the dandelion tincture. "This will help with your headache right away," she said, "and if you let Dandy sprinkle some fairy dust over you, the healing will go even faster."

The Old Man agreed. After he'd taken some of the tincture and Dandy had added fairy dust, he lay back down and closed his eyes.

Hailey turned to the May Queen. "I'd like to make some teas for him," she said. "Can you help me?"

The May Queen led Hailey into the kitchen and Sarah and Camie followed, eager to help with the medicine making. Dandy and Rowan stayed behind to watch over the Old Man.

Camie and Sarah looked on as Hailey began her preparations. She put four ounces of dried dandelion root into a pan and added two quarts of water. She brought this to a boil while at the same time heating some water for tea. When the water came to a boil, she turned down the heat on the pot with the dandelion root and let it simmer gently. "We'll let that go for about twenty minutes," she said. "Until half the water boils away."

"That's a decoction, isn't it, Hailey?" Sarah asked.

"That's right," said Hailey. "Good memory. It's a good way to extract medicine from harder plant material, like roots."

"I can just pour this water over the leaves to make the tea for his fever, right?" asked Camie.

"Yep," said Hailey. "We'll use some of the dried leaves that Dandy gave us, because more of the medicine will be available that way since the cell walls have been broken down."

Camie poured the hot water into the cup over the leaves and they covered the cup with a small plate to let the tea steep.

When they turned around, they found that the May Queen was quietly weeping while they worked.

Sarah went to her side. "What is it?" she asked. "Are you worried about the Old Man of the Forest?"

The May Queen nodded. "I'm also just feeling so grateful that you're here, and that he's letting you help. I don't know how he's ever going to be able to forgive himself, though."

Sarah nodded and gave the May Queen a hug. "We'll just take it one step at a time," she said. "That's what we did with each of the magic keepers, and somehow I think that with all of us working together we'll be able to help him."

The May Queen gave a small smile, but she still looked doubtful.

"You know," said Hailey, "we should probably cook up all the fresh roots and greens we gathered too, since the Old Man of the Forest is so tired and weak. There's so much deep nourishment in dandelions. I know it will help him feel better."

"I'll make a stir fry," said Camie, eager for a kitchen project.

"Perfect," said Hailey.

They all worked together to wash and chop up the plants they'd gathered.

"Should we put the flowers in too?" Camie asked.

"Let's make some fritters with them," said Hailey. "He'll probably like them dipped in honey. The stir fry will be bitter, and it will be nice for him to have something sweet too."

"Let's make a bouquet to put by the Old Man's bed first," said Sarah. "Remember how being in that field of flowers cheered us all up. I bet the sunny yellow bouquet will help the Old Man feel better."

"Great idea!" said Camie.

The May Queen brought out a vase and when the flowers had been arranged in it she took it to the Old Man's bedside, where he would see it when he woke up.

By the time Camie had finished making the stir fry and the fritters, the decoction had finished steeping.

"Let's mix some of the root decoction in with the leaf tea," Hailey suggested. "Then we won't have to try to get him to drink two different medicine teas." She added some honey to the tea, knowing it would be bitter. "I'd add some milk or cream too if we had it," she said. "My dad drinks dandelion root tea instead of coffee sometimes, and he's let me try it with cream and honey. It tastes really good."

The girls prepared a tray with the food and the tea and brought it to the Old Man's bedside. The May Queen gently

ran her hand over the Old Man's brow and gave him a kiss on the forehead to wake him up. He awoke looking into her eyes, and a smile lit up his face, but then he seemed to remember everything and his face closed up once more.

"How does your head feel?" the May Queen asked.

"It feels...it feels better." There was wonder in the Old Man's voice. He looked at Dandy and the children, and they could see the gratitude in his eyes. "Oh, it's been hurting so much," he said. "I couldn't think straight at all."

"We made you some lunch," said Camie.

The Old Man looked at the tray doubtfully.

"I know you may not feel much like eating," said Sarah. "Try some of the tea first. It will help with your fever, and then it's important to get some good food into your body. You can't fully heal when you're so tired and weak."

The Old Man noticed the bouquet of flowers next to the tray and he looked at them for a long time. "Okay, okay," he said, giving in to Sarah's coaxing. He took a sip of the tea, and then a longer drink. "Oh," he said. "That seems like just what I need right now. It's bitter, but it tastes so good."

Dandy sprinkled the Old Man with some more fairy dust, and when Sarah touched his brow, she could tell the fever had broken.

"You know," said the Old Man, "I am starting to feel kind of hungry." He ate some of the stir fry and dipped a fritter into the honey. He actually smiled after his first bite of fritter. "These are delicious!" he said. He ate a few more bites, but then sat back on the bed. "I think that's all I can do for now."

"That's more than he's eaten in days," said the May Queen, smiling.

"You know," said the Old Man of the Forest, "I seem to be remembering something. A riddle, I think."

"Really," said Camie. "Do you think it's a riddle for us to guess your name?"

The Old Man considered. "Yes," he said. "Yes, I think it is. Listen. I have an 'I' at my center, but most often my name encourages you to look beyond yourself."

"Wow," said Camie. "You must have a magic keeper name too!"

"How are you feeling?" asked Hailey. "Do you think you could walk to the Fairy Herb Garden? Healing happens so much faster there."

"Maybe," said the Old Man, but he sounded doubtful. "I do feel a bit stronger after the food, but my joints have been so sore. I think I'm getting arthritis in my old age. I haven't been able to walk too well."

Hailey brought out the dandelion flower–infused oil. "This should help with the arthritis," she said. All the children helped to rub the oil into the Old Man's joints, and Dandy sprinkled fairy dust over him when they were finished.

"Ohhhhhhhh. Ahhhhhhh," said the Old Man as they worked. "That feels amazing!" He began to flex his knees and elbows, twirl his ankles and wrists, and bend his fingers and toes. "I didn't realize how much pain I was in until it went away. My mind is getting so much clearer. I'm remembering another part of the riddle! When you are living in my name, it is impossible to be unhappy."

"A mansion," Rowan guessed. He loved the outdoors, but still dreamed of living in a fancy house someday.

"Hawaii," said Hailey. She'd loved their vacation to the Hawaiian beaches a few years before.

"Disneyland?" Camie ventured, thinking how happy her family had been riding the Disneyland rides.

"Hmmmm," said Sarah. "I don't see how any of those have an 'I' in the middle. I think we're going to need the last clue."

"Do you think you can make it to the Fairy Herb Garden now?" Hailey asked.

The Old Man bowed his head. "I don't think I can face the fairies," he said. "Or any of the magic keepers really."

"I have an idea!" said Dandy, and before they could ask what it was, he'd flown right out the door.

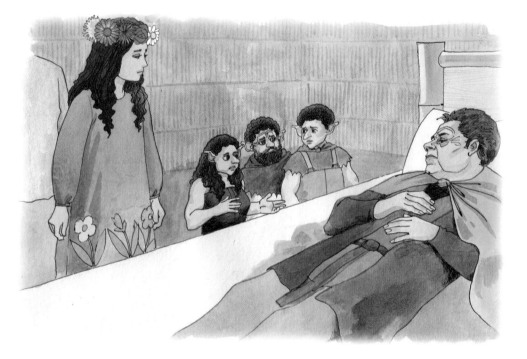

CHAPTER 5
Forgiveness

Dandy brought the magic keepers back with him. Well, he'd brought the trolls, anyway, and had sent for the others. Trust, Awareness, and Inspiration came and stood by the Old Man's bed. He bowed his head, avoiding their eyes.

Trust spoke first. She put a hand on the Old Man's shoulder. "It was a very bad thing that you did, casting that spell," she said. "It was bad because it resulted in a lot of suffering. I remember how it was in the time before you cast the spell, though. It was hard and confusing for all of us. The humans were turning away from the plants and doing things none of us understood. I know how their thoughtless actions in the forest hurt your soul. You were angry, and we all do things we later regret when we're angry. We have a chance now, though. A chance to put all the suffering behind us, a chance to work together in new ways. The May Queen's spell has reconnected us with the humans, and we have magic keepers among them now. Perhaps in some way, your actions were just part of something larger that needed to happen. Like my name, I tend to trust that everything is happening just the way it needs to. I want you to know that I forgive you."

The Old Man looked up then, warily, into the troll's eyes. "I forgive you," she repeated.

"Thank you," he whispered. "Thank you, Trust."

Awareness came forward. "I think we're all more aware after this experience," he said. "We're aware of how important the magic is, how important we all are to each other, aware of so many things that we used to take for granted. I see the gifts that have come out of all of this. I wish we could have gained those gifts in a different way, a way that didn't require so much suffering, but still I'm thankful for the gifts. Here we are in this present moment, and like Trust I see a chance for us to move forward in a new and amazing way. I see that the first step is forgiveness and find that in my heart I truly do feel forgiveness for you."

Inspiration spoke next. "Thank you for allowing the children to heal you, for being courageous, and taking that step toward a better future. That, sir, is inspiring. If I allow myself to get caught up in the past I can be resentful and upset, but when I stand here in this room with these brave, clever children, with my fellow troll magic keepers, with the May Queen awake and among us once more, and with you taking steps toward renewed health, I feel hopeful. I feel inspired about what the future might hold. Like the others, I am sad that our path here had to be so challenging, but I too find it is in my heart to forgive you, Old Man—to forgive and move forward to create an inspiring future together."

For a moment the Old Man's eyes sparkled with hope as Inspiration spoke of an inspiring future. "Thank you," said the Old Man. "Thank you all, but when I look at you and think of all I put you through, I just can't stand it. I hate myself so much. I feel like I want to run away from myself, but no matter how far I run, I can't get away from me. I can't get away from my shame. And I'm afraid. Afraid that if I forgive myself I might do it again—act out of anger, I mean."

The elf magic keepers arrived next—Play, Knowledge, and Beauty. Rowan was relieved to see that they all looked healthy. He'd been worried since their walk through the forest.

Play came forward first. "Old Man," she said, "as beings of the forest we are perhaps closer to your heart than any. These years when the forest has been ill have been devastating for all of us. There has been no joy, no play in us, but now we have a chance, a chance for health and playfulness. I know that you were angry when you cast that spell, and

that it was your anger that blinded you. I see and feel how you have suffered too, through all these years. How you are suffering now. The whole forest feels it. But you have a chance now to choose life. To learn from your mistake, to move us all forward toward a future filled with a new level of cooperation and play. After all that's happened, I don't think you'll ever act out of anger again."

"Indeed," said Knowledge, "these events have given you the knowledge and insight you've needed to grow to a place where you will not again act hastily."

"You will choose beauty," said Beauty. "I would trust that from you more than anyone else, because of all you've been through."

When the dwarf magic keepers arrived, Love came forward, to the Old Man's bedside. "Old man," he said, "you stole my children's childhoods from me. Years that could have been spent in the joy of watching them grow were instead spent in torment, trying to find a way to release the magic from that infernal puzzle box."

The Old Man wanted to look away as Love spoke, but he felt he could not do so, not after what this magic keeper had lost. He owed it to the dwarf to look him squarely in the eye. "Yes," he said. "I'm sorry. I'm so very sorry." It felt good to say it. He was surprised to find that it felt good to take responsibility for what he'd done, almost like it released a weight from his shoulders.

"I know that you are," said Love. "I know that if you could, you would give me those years back. I am proud to be a magic keeper for my people," he said. "I am proud of the life I have lived. And, after all, my name is Love. I cannot help but love. Even after all you've done, I love you, and I forgive you."

"Look at how we're coming together," said Consensus. "Loving and forgiving. Your spell may have caused terrible suffering, but it also helped the dwarves remember their friendship with the mountain giant and the fairies, and I see the way it is helping us all build new levels of trust. I too forgive you, Old Man."

"And I," said Celebration. "Your spell led me on some amazing adventures. I actually found the land of the unicorns. Can you imagine?" Her eyes lit up as she said the word unicorn. The children remembered their magical ride on the unicorn's back and they couldn't help but smile. "I forgive you, Old Man."

The brownies came next—Compassion, Reflection, and Simplicity. Compassion stepped forward and looked into the Old Man's eyes. He didn't speak, but the Old Man saw pure compassion reflected back at him. He felt completely understood.

When Reflection looked into his eyes, the Old Man saw himself clearly. He saw how his beating heart was connected to the life of the forest and the elves. He saw himself as a young man, the forest prince, walking through the forest in absolute awe of its beauty. He saw his anger when the humans cut down the trees without giving thanks for the lives they were taking. He saw his confusion when they stopped looking to the plants for healing help. He saw the moment when he cast his terrible spell. He saw his shame and his fear and for a moment his courage almost failed him. He began to look away, but his eyes passed over the elves, beings of his very heart, and he forced himself to look up again. He faced his shame and fear squarely. He allowed himself to feel it. All of it. When he did he cried out, a great cry of anguish that rang through the forest.

Simplicity's eyes showed the heart of it: his sickness, the dying forest, and then his healing, the children helping him, and the restoration of the elves' health and the vibrancy returning to his beloved trees. They showed his courage

now, facing his shame, feeling his feelings, and taking responsibility.

He looked around at all the Magic Keepers, so generous in their offerings of forgiveness. He looked at the children, so willing to help him heal with the help of the plant magic. He looked at Dandy, with his charming, boyish smile, and finally, he looked at the May Queen. He felt his love for her course through his veins. He saw how tired she looked, and looked down at his own old, tired body.

"I can feel your hope," he said, "and I want to forgive myself, I really do, but I feel so sad. I can't believe what we've all had to go through, and to think of myself and the part I played..." His voice trailed off, and tears ran again down his face.

Hailey touched her flower crown to give herself the confidence she needed to speak. "I know what you need," she said, and everyone turned toward her. "You need one last bit of dandelion medicine. Come," she said, "follow me." She left him no room to refuse this time, but simply took Rowan's hand and led the way out the door. "Help me get him to the dandelion patch," she whispered to her big brother as they left the cabin.

CHAPTER 6
A Magical Walk

Astonishing even himself, the Old Man rose from his bed, stood, and did exactly as Hailey had asked. He followed her, this brave little girl with such a gift for healing. He followed her, and everyone else followed him. It was quite a parade of magical creatures on that forest path that day.

Rowan guided Hailey, and as was often the case, the walk back to the dandelion patch seemed to take much less time than their walk to the Old Man's cabin. When they got there, Hailey motioned to the Old Man to go into the patch.

"What?" he asked. "Where's the medicine?"

"You'll see," said Hailey. "You'll see. Just walk through the flowers."

Sarah remembered how happy they all felt earlier when they were among the dandelion flowers in that field, how they couldn't stop laughing, and she had an idea what Hailey was doing.

The Old Man shook his head doubtfully, but stepped forward nonetheless. He began to walk among the flowers. Then he found himself bending down to touch them. He even picked one and ate it. He ran his hands over the tops of them. As he did so, something amazing began to happen inside him. All his sorrow, all his doubts, began to melt away. He felt  himself smiling, not just with his lips, but with his whole body, and then the smile tumbled out of his mouth and he was laughing.

As he continued his walk through the dandelions, those looking on witnessed an incredible transformation. Years slipped from the shoulders of the Old Man. He stood up straighter, his thin shoulders became broad, and his chest filled out to a strong roundness. When he emerged from the dandelions he was no longer the Old Man of the Forest. This man had claimed his birthright at last. With the help of the dandelions, he had transformed his anger, his fear, his shame, and his sadness into wisdom. He was in body and mind the Forest King.

Hailey, Rowan, Sarah, and Camie held up a crown of woven dandelion flowers and he took it from them and placed it on his head. "I've remembered the final clue of the riddle," he said. "My name is another word for appreciation, and offering me to others is one of the best gifts you can give."

The children looked at one another, and found they hardly had to think about the clues at all. They all knew the answer, and they looked up at the Forest King and said, "Gratitude. Your name is Gratitude!"

"So it is, so it is," he said wonderingly. "And today I am filled up with gratitude, so much so that I would like to grant you a wish. We can do that, can't we?" he asked the May Queen.

"Indeed we can," she said as she stepped forward to take his hand. The two smiled at each other, a smile of pure love and pure light, and the forest behind them shimmered and glowed with vibrant beauty. "Why don't you four talk over your wish as we walk back to the Fairy Herb Garden. We must honor you with more than a wish, I think."

The whole magical entourage then made their way through the dandelions, smiling and talking and laughing all the way. As they walked up the hill toward the Fairy Herb Garden, the four children whispered together, trying to agree on a wish.

When they arrived at the garden they gathered at the May Pole, the only place with enough open space for the larger creatures to enter without disturbing fairy homes. Dandy flew from fairy house to fairy house announcing the arrival of the May Queen and the Forest King. Fairies flocked from all corners of the garden to see this couple restored to health.

While the fairies gathered, turning aerial somersaults of happiness around the Forest King, Camie touched the arm of the May Queen. "I was just wondering," she said. "Do you have a magic keeper name? I mean, it seems like you must be a magic keeper as well."

The May Queen smiled down at Camie. "Why yes," she said. "Yes, I do."

Looking up into the face of the May Queen, Camie could see that her magic keeper name would include all of the other names. She was love and beauty and compassion...all of them wrapped into one.

"My name," said the May Queen, "is Wonder."

"And like I am the heart of the forest," said the Forest King, "she is the heart of the whole beautiful spinning world."

The fairies made a great circle around all the magic keepers, and the May Queen whispered to the children to stand with the race for whom they'd accepted the role of magic keeper.

Hailey found herself in the east with the trolls, Rowan was in the south with the elves, Camie in the west with the dwarves, and Sarah in the north with the brownies. The May Queen and the Forest King came to each of them in turn.

"Hailey," said the May Queen, "thank you for all of your healing help. Thank you for using your gifts to help restore the magic to the world. Thank you for becoming a magic keeper for the trolls. May your life be blessed with trust, awareness, and inspiration."

"Rowan," said the Forest King, "thank you for using your wilderness skills and all of your gifts to help restore the magic to the world. Thank you for becoming a magic keeper for the elves. May your life be blessed with play, knowledge, and beauty."

"Camie," said the May Queen, "thank you for your clarity. Your ability to see the good in everyone and all of your gifts have helped restore the magic to the world. Thank you for becoming a magic keeper for the dwarves. May your life be blessed with love, consensus, and celebration."

"Sarah," said the Forest King, "thank you for your caring ways and your loving, soothing voice and for willingly using all your gifts to help restore the magic to the world. Thank you for becoming a magic keeper for the brownies. May your life be blessed with compassion, reflection, and simplicity."

A great whoop of joy went up from the circle of fairies when the May Queen and the Forest King finished offering their gratitude to the children. All of them clapped and laughed and flipped and cheered.

The May Queen and the Forest King gathered the children into the center of the circle and asked them what wish they would like to have granted. The children looked at one another and smiled. They'd thought about all sorts of wishes—like trying to make sure the magic never faded from the world again, or wishing they could come to fairyland whenever they wanted, or wishing for fortunes, or to live forever—but they knew from reading so many story books that wishes like that never seemed to work out quite the way they were intended, so in the end they decided to go with Hailey's very simple wish. Rowan gave Hailey a nudge, encouraging her to tell their wish.

"We wish," said Hailey, "we wish we could be fairy size and have wings like the fairies just for one day, just until we go home," she said.

The May Queen smiled at Hailey and held hands with the Forest King. Together they lifted their arms and spoke some words in a language more musical and beautiful even than the

elvish they'd heard, and then the fairies sprinkled them with fairy dust, and they felt the familiar tingling and shrinking, and then something else, right between their shoulder blades. They felt a bulging, pushing feeling, and then they watched each other in amazement as beautiful, golden fairy wings sprouted from their backs.

They found they could flex their wings as easily as they could lift their arms or use their legs to walk. They flew joyfully into the air, and soared around the Fairy Herb Garden.

"I wish my little sister, Lizzy, could be here to fly with us," Camie told Hailey. And suddenly, there she was, Lizzy with fairy wings of her own, smiling and flying with her big sister.

They did aerial flips and dives and rolls. The fairies joined them, of course, showing them new moves and tricks. The May Queen and the Forest King and all of the magic keepers looked on in delight.

Whatever was going to happen next, today was a day for pure joy, and those four children learning to use their brand new wings and flying among their fairy friends were a living embodiment of the great happiness they all felt inside. Today, the healing of the world was truly complete.

Glossary

Fritters (frit-ers): A piece of fruit, vegetable, meat, (or flower) that is coated in batter and deep-fried.

What's Next?

Learn more about dandelion in the Herb Fairies member area!

After you complete the Magic Keeper's Journal, color Dandy, make some recipes, and print out a picture of him for your wall. Learn lots more about dandelion in Herbal Roots Zine, which has recipes, puzzles, activities, stories, songs and more!

Psssst... One last surprise! →

CONGRATULATIONS MAGIC KEEPER!

You've finished the *Herb Fairies* series and right along with Hailey, Rowan, Camie, and Sarah you've been learning about the healing power of plants. By now your own *Magic Keeper's Journal* is full of the pages you've completed. Like Sarah's magic book, your journal will always be there to help you remember all that you've learned.

But magic keepers don't keep their knowledge to themselves, do they?

Now, it's time for you to share what you know. Make a cup of pine needle tea for your mom or dad when they're sick so they get that extra vitamin C. Tell your friends about using plantain poultices on their bee stings and chickweed on their cuts.

And, don't stop learning! You can add even more pages to your *Magic Keeper's Journal*. There are many wonderful books about the healing plants. Ask your parents to help you find some that you like. Keep reading and keep experimenting with herbal remedies and recipes. The plants will become like trusted friends and allies and together we will keep the plant magic alive and working in our world.

Have fun sharing the magic!
Kimberly

Author Kimberly Gallagher, M.Ed. is also creator of *Wildcraft!, An Herbal Adventure Game*, by LearningHerbs.com. Her Masters in Education is from Antioch University in Seattle, and she taught at alternative schools in the Puget Sound region. Kimberly has extensive training in non-violent communication and conflict resolution. Her love of nature, writing, teaching, gardening, herbs, fantasy books and storytelling led her to create Herb Fairies.

alchemy
OF HERBS

TRANSFORM

EVERYDAY

INGREDIENTS INTO

FOODS & REMEDIES

THAT HEAL

ROSALEE
DE LA FORÊT

FOREWORD BY
ROSEMARY GLADSTAR

Available at your favorite bookseller.
Brought to you by LearningHerbs & Hay House Publishing.

Download Herb Fairies coloring pages in the member area.

Not a member? Visit HerbFairies.com.